Laila's Lion
and Stories from Other Cultures

Stories by
Chris Ashley, Kathryn White,
Elizabeth Laird and Ruskin Bond

Illustrations by
Alan Marks, David Dean, Tim Clarey
and Neil Reed

Contents

Laila's Lion

Written by
Chris Ashley

Illustrated by Alan Marks

CHAPTER ONE

The African sun beat down on the roof of the railway carriage, and underneath, the creature prowled. There was a noise, a snuffle, as it found the gap in the rotting wood, and then a scratching at the carriage floor. It had found the man scent.

Laila usually ran up the steps to her grandparents' house, but today her feet just slurped up the concrete steps. January slush sent pangs of cold through her soaking socks, and something else sent the same sort of pain into her chest. It hurt.

It could have been a back to school hurting, seeing all that was left of Christmas sticking out of the big yellow dustbins. But it wasn't.

It could have been that last week was the Christmas holiday with parties and visitors and this week was wet breaks and school dinners. It could have been, but it wasn't.

It was the same sort of pain that had gripped her when blonde-haired, blue-eyed Louise got the star part in Cinderella, and Laila had ended up with a minor part in the ball scene. Laila had secretly hoped that

Cinderella would miss the ball with the flu that was going round. Yes, Laila knew exactly what the pain was. It was shame, and now she was feeling it again. Laila Mahe was ashamed.

Grandpa answered her angry raps on the letter box, and when he saw her, his eyes softened and his old face broke into a young boy's grin. Laila glared past him to the fluorescent yellow coat on the banister. She saw that Grandpa had seen her look, and now it hurt even more. Laila was ashamed of being ashamed.

She was ashamed that she'd pretended her hands were too cold to come out of her pockets to hold his hand that morning, ashamed of staying on at homework club rather than walk home with him after school, and ashamed of knowing that the milk letter was the only one she'd be handing in that night. The one inviting Grandpa to talk to the class tomorrow was staying in her pocket.

Laila loved Grandpa more than anything. But he was the new lollipop lady, and Laila was ashamed.

CHAPTER TWO

They huddled inside the carriage, both shaking. The older boy with fever, the younger with pure fear. They'd heard about the creature, and they knew what it wanted. They would have to move. It was a desperate struggle for the younger one, but he did it. He dragged his sick brother away from the pawing underneath, and into a corner where the wood was stronger, and where the metal wheel could stop a mighty paw from swiping its way through the old timber.

Then, sweating but not breathing, he listened … Nothing. Out there in the bush, where the birds and the insects performed a deafening symphony, there was never really 'nothing'. But to the boy, listening only for one thing, there wasn't a sound. Nothing. And that was worse.

Laila hung her coat so that she couldn't see the shiny yellow one. Then she smelt her way into the kitchen, where before today, her two worlds had always mixed into one really happy one.

Grandpa and Grandma had been born in the Seychelles, and moved to Britain before Laila's mum had been born. But despite the years, the miles, and the weather, Laila's family always managed to bring some of their tropical paradise to the cold city, especially to the kitchen.

A huge calendar of scenes from the Seychelles dominated the wall. From the calendar, water twinkled and bowing palm trees guarded empty stretches of white sand. On the work surface, next to *Shoppers' Weekly* and a hot water bottle, was a coconut grown in his own garden by Uncle Joshua. But it was the smells that really did it. Smells of dishes that made you forget school with your first sniff … usually!

'Yes, it's Laila … Come on woman.' Grandpa was winding her up now. 'She needs some food. She's had a hard day.'

'Oh shut up you old *couillon*!' Grandma laughed. She still used the Creole word for a fool.

'Come on, Laila … What do you want?' Grandpa was clanging pans. 'Curry, lentils … I know …' And his face lit up in pure joy. '*Ladoab*, your favourite. Ladoab for Laila.' He clanged some more, muttering to himself as he began emptying the fridge. 'Ladoab. Where is the ladoab?'

'It's all right. I'll have toast.'

But Grandpa was on a mission. 'Ladoab … It's her favourite … Back home when I came in from school …'

But Grandma had had enough, and Grandpa was pushed chuckling to his armchair. 'Go and sit down, couillon! I'll give her ladoab.'

Grandma made the sign of the cross towards the picture of the Holy Mother that hung on the kitchen wall, and bustled in silence while the smell of sweet potato ladoab cooking eased Laila's mind, and took her away from Natasha, Annabelle and Scott.

But when she went into the front room and saw Grandpa snoring, she thought how old he suddenly looked, and the pain in her chest came straight back as she thought of 5T and Grandpa's first day as the lollipop lady.

'Hey, Laila, is the new lollipop lady really your granddad? ... Cool hat!'

A few laughs.

'I bet he holds Laila's hand to cross the front room.'

Big laughs.

Then Scott had whispered something else. Some had laughed, some hadn't, but they'd all looked at her, and Laila knew who it was about.

During Art it got whispered some more. It reached Laila's group. Natasha had laughed, but it was when she whispered it to Annabelle, Laila's best friend, that they'd been caught.

'And what's so funny, Red Group?'

Silence.

'Come on, tell us.'

Annabelle had gone scarlet. 'It's a joke, Miss. Scott told us it.' Scott had a helper for his behaviour, and blaming him for something usually got you off the hook.

'Oh well then ... Come on, Annabelle. Give us all a laugh.' Mrs Thomas, in her Christmas jumper, was in a good mood and was joining in. But Annabelle just stared at the table.

'Come on, Annabelle.'

Annabelle looked up briefly while the

rest of those that knew it waited, loving every second. Laila waited too. Annabelle glanced at her and then whispered something.

'Come on, Annabelle.'

Annabelle croaked a bit louder. 'What's …' She stopped again, and again she looked at Laila. 'What's yellow and black, and carries a warning?'

'Ooh, I'm good at these.' Miss put on a puzzled face. 'Um, I know – a dangerous wasp!'

There was no answer.

'Annabelle?'

'No.'

'A bee? A hornet?'

'No.'

'Come on then, what?'

Annabelle had looked around at everyone staring at her. Everyone apart from one person. 'I've forgotten, Miss.'

There was a thirty-person breathe out and shouting from Mrs Thomas.

'Well it couldn't have been very funny could it, Annabelle? Come here and show me what you've done so far, and just work in silence if you've got nothing sensible to say.'

It was when she'd come back from the desk that Jennifer, who hadn't heard it, dared ask her. 'What's the answer?' she'd whispered. And Annabelle whispered it. Laila never heard properly, and for all she knew it could have been something about a wasp. But deep down she was sure, sure she'd heard that it was, 'Laila's granddad, yellow and black'.

Now, curled up on the sofa, Laila could still hear the sniggers and still feel Annabelle's cold stare. She looked across to where Grandpa was snoring and she tried not to be cross with him. But why did he have to be a stupid lollipop lady? Why couldn't he just be … normal?

CHAPTER THREE

The older boy managed to lift his head enough to stare into the face of the younger one. Just that one look told him. It wasn't another one of the tricks that his fever had sent to rush around his head. The terror in his brother's face was real. It was down there. It had come for them.

He pointed to the pile of kit by the door. 'Gun,' he whispered. The younger boy searched, but there was no gun. And now the snuffling and scratching began again as the lion's claws raked at the rotten wood of the carriage floor. But the younger boy was staring desperately at a shaft of light coming from the sliding door – the door was open …

Laila held it all in until Mum came to pick her up. Then she just couldn't stop the tears, and her words came out in such sobs that Mum had to stop the car.

Laila told her about everything then – Annabelle, the teasing, and the yellow and black joke.

'Why does he have to be a stupid lollipop lady anyway?'

'Crossing Patrol,' Mum said calmly.

And then as the talking helped the pain out, Laila remembered when she'd had the feeling before …

'And why can't you have a black Cinderella?'

'Who said you can't?' Mum was angry now, really angry.

Laila didn't know. It was someone behind her at the auditions, but that was where she knew her hurting from.

'I know, I know,' Mum murmured, rocking her. But she didn't. She hadn't been there today, had she?

'Why do we have to be different?' Laila whispered almost to herself, and that made Mum angry again.

'Would you really want to be the same as everybody else?'

Laila thought about it … Yes she would! In Year Five you had to be the same – same trainers, same bag, same hair, same friends. You couldn't be different. But grown ups didn't understand that sort of thing, so Laila just shook her head.

'And anyway,' Mum said, 'there's another word for different.'

'What's that?' Laila mumbled.

'Special. And that's our family – special.'

Special. Laila looked out of the car window. The more she thought about it, the more she knew that she was doing the right thing keeping the letter. She'd had enough of 'special'.

Look, cover, write, check … Laila finished her spellings and pretended not to care that Annabelle had moved to sit next to Natasha.

Work diary. Numeracy, page 17. Division with Mrs Thomas. Literacy. Set out interview questions for visitors.

'What visitors, Miss?' someone asked.

And Miss explained while Laila sat holding her breath. They were all going to practise interview questions by having a class visit from Natasha's granddad, because he had been evacuated during the war and the war was their topic.

'And I've asked Laila's grandfather, Mr Mahe, the new lo … the new Crossing Patrol, to come and be interviewed about his job.'

Laila waited. Nothing at first.

Sensible questions in jotters. What was an air raid shelter like? Were you ever scared?

But Laila didn't have to wait long. Scott's helper, Miss Nolan, moved off to help someone else and it started, Natasha pretending to write eagerly.

'What do lollipop ladies have in their sandwiches?'

'Traffic jam!'

There were laughs and then whispers.

'What's white and black and carries a lollipop?'

'A zebra on its summer holiday.'

Laila breathed out. She could take that one.

Then Scott again. 'What's yellow and black and carries a lollipop?'

Nobody said anything, but Laila caught a glance between Annabelle and Natasha and just picked up her stuff and moved to the writers' corner. Thank goodness she hadn't given Grandpa the letter. They'd all be laughing, even Annabelle. Annabelle, who in the good times, spent nearly as long at Grandma and Grandpa's as Laila did.

'Are you OK, Laila?'

'Yes, Miss.'

No!

'Got any questions for Granddad?'

'No, Miss.'

Yes. Why couldn't he have just been an evacuee?

CHAPTER FOUR

*Seconds. That was all there could be before the
lion found the door open and … The boy stood
up. It was up to him to get to the other side of
the carriage and close it. The older one could
only look on, helpless. The boy made his move,
and there was a roar that set the branches
cracking and the birds to flight. They would
return when it was over.*

The hall still smelt of cottage pie, and there
was still a piece of tinsel over the door. They
were all sitting there with clipboards and
pencils, and Mrs Thomas was telling them
how lucky they were to have a visit from Mr
Purvis, and …

Laila put her hand up. She'd tell them
now so that there was no chance for
questions before Natasha's granddad got
started. Grandpa was ill, she'd say. Sorry he
couldn't come.

But then Mrs Nix, the headteacher, led
in a tall grey-haired man with a moustache,
a checked jacket, and a handkerchief, the
same red colour as his face, sticking out of
his top pocket. Just the sort of granddad

you got in reading books. She was leading in somebody else, too.

The other man wore a shiny yellow coat with two silver fluorescent lines, and it would have been hard to tell what was working hardest, Laila's eyes popping, or her ears straining for giggles behind her.

'Yes, Laila.'

Laila hadn't realised that her hand was still up, but Grandpa saw her and gave a great wink. She turned her hand into a half wave, and then grasped the letter in her pocket and looked at it. *Milk will cost £1.20 per week. Please sign below if …* Laila looked up, and there was Grandpa with another letter, *the* letter, in his own hand. He winked again.

'What was it like in an air raid shelter?'

'Well, it was dark of course,' replied Mr Purvis, 'and damp … pretty cold.'

Pencils raced across clipboards. Mrs Thomas looked pleased.

'Robert?'

'What was it like being bombed?'

'Well, er …' Mr Purvis buffed his nose with his great handkerchief. 'I was never actually bombed, of course.'

A groan from the floor. Disappointment.

'... because, of course, I was evacuated out to the country.'

Mr Purvis answered all of their questions, and Mrs Thomas said what sensible ones they had been. Scott and Tyler were the only people who had to be sent out, and there were only a few shushes when children started whispering. They all clapped, and Tyler and Scott were brought back in to sit at the front by Mrs Nix.

'Well, those of you that cross at the main entrance will already know Mr Mahe. He is our Crossing Patrol. Mr Mahe, would you like to answer some questions about your very important work?'

Laila could already hear the sniggers.

Hands were up, but she only had one question – Why her? And she looked at her clipboard so hard it should have broken.

Richard asked the first one. Good old Richard, he tried hard.

'How long have you been a lollipop man?'

'Two days.'

They all laughed, properly, not nastily, and Laila liked Richard, she really liked him.

'Before that I worked on the railways. I retired just before Christmas.'

'Ooh, do you know Thomas the Tank Engine?' It was Natasha, whispered and nasty.

Belinda was supposed to be next, but Scott was making so many me, me, me noises that Miss let him have a go. He stood up, opened his jotter, and turned around to make sure that he had a full audience. Then he read his question slowly and deliberately, just as he had scribed it down with Miss Nolan.

'Were … you … ever … scared in your shelter?'

The hall erupted into laughter. Trust Scott. Not listening as usual, and sent out when he should have asked it. He'd got the wrong visitor.

'I think that was for Mr Purvis, wasn't it, Scott?' And Scott, standing up in front of everybody laughing at him, suddenly wasn't so big. He didn't have a joke to get out of this, and he was turning the same red colour as Mr Purvis. Laila should have been enjoying it. He'd started it. He'd made the joke about Grandpa that had got her laughed at and made her different. But it was horrible seeing Scott in distress up there, and she was pleased when somebody saved him.

'Oh, I think I can answer that, Scott.' Grandpa stood up over the laughter and gave one of his Grandpa winks. 'Yes, really, really scared. Shall I just tell you or let everyone hear?'

Scott looked around, a little of his power and dignity back. 'Everyone,' he said to a great cheer. But he didn't half sit down quickly.

The old man took off his yellow coat, and in his own time hung it proudly on the back of his chair. Grandpa had taken over.

CHAPTER FIVE

The boy closed his eyes as he reached for the door. Would it be claw or teeth through that gap? Push! Push! But the door wouldn't budge. He knelt down and tried to force the bottom, and when he dared to look, he found himself staring into two amber eyes.

Panic gave the boy a surge of power, but the door stayed stuck fast. Open it a bit wider! Force it past the sticky bit! He tugged and the door moved. But instead of opening a few centimetres it flew along its track, and opened wide with a bang that shuddered the whole carriage. Close it! Close it! But that door wasn't budging again. And before the creature could move, the boy glanced back at his brother, jumped through the open door, and ran. The lion would have to choose.

Grandpa started, boring at first. How he'd left school at fourteen and gone to Nairobi in Kenya, Africa. How he got a job fixing trains – great old steam trains as big as the hall. Then how they wanted to build a railway line down through Kenya and Tanzania, and link up with the south of Africa. How he had to be up at the front, keeping the great locomotive going, as mile upon mile of track was laid down. It was boring and Laila cringed. Didn't he know what he was doing to her?

'What's so frightening about that?' someone wanted to know.

'It was Africa!' Grandpa shouted it then whispered it. 'Antelopes, wildebeest, zebra …

snakes.' Grandpa walked up and down the rows, and most of the whispering stopped.

'In the second week, the snakes took four men.'

All of the whispering stopped, and the first clipboards dropped. Every neck craned to follow Grandpa's movement. Suddenly he froze.

'What creatures kill more people than any other in Africa?'

'Lions.'

'No.'

'Snakes?'

'No. The hippo. We surprised a hippo and it chased us. We were lucky, the local villagers trapped it for us, and we ate hippo. Ever eaten hippo, Scott?'

'No.' Scott was kneeling up, concentrating in the hall for the first time since reception class.

'Don't. Very fatty, very sour … By the end of the third week, they'd cleared enough trees for us to get one more track down before a break for the weekend. One tree was in the way, and some of our boys decided not to wait for the locals. They went at it themselves to try and get home early. Big mistake my friends. It was a bee tree.

African bees that sting until you drop.
Another five of us sent back to Nairobi.'

'Did you get stung?'

'No. I was lucky. I was with the engine,
and they didn't like the smoke and steam.
But something bit me, a mosquito.'

The hall was silent except for Grandpa's
voice, and even Laila had forgotten
everything to listen to the story.

Grandpa told how they'd carried on chopping and burning their way through the bush, how one day the villagers had stopped coming, and the work had halted.

He told them how it was his job to stay and keep the fire heating the boiler of the great locomotive, and how his mosquito bite had suddenly made him hotter and hotter, until he was so dizzy he couldn't stand.

They cheered when they heard that Grandpa's brother, Baptiste, on school holidays, had made the journey up the tracks to look after him in one of the old railway carriages.

Then Grandpa told them why the villagers had stopped coming, and there was a gasp. A lion had taken somebody who had gone too far from the fire … and now it had the taste … the people taste … and the people smell … and it knew it was easy.

Laila felt a tight grip on her arm. It was Natasha, not trying to hurt, just gripping, and Laila knew that Mum had been right. She was different. Different because she had her grandpa.

She looked up and saw Natasha's granddad listening. His mouth open too.

Every family had their stories, they were all different. But as Laila listened to her grandpa's story, she was glad to be different, to have stories like this. Mum was right, she was special. They were special.

'Scott, do you know when I was most scared?'

Scott just shook his head.

'It was when I realised that he was under our railway carriage. I was dizzy with the fever, but I could feel something tickling. It was his mane, coming through the wood. Then I could smell him, smell his cat's smell, smell his warm fur, and smell his terrible breath. And then my brother dragged me to a stronger part of the carriage.'

Grandpa went on to explain how Baptiste had looked in the kit for a gun ... but there was no gun, how they realised the door was slightly open, and how Baptiste had tried to close it, and in doing so had come face to face with the lion, and had run.

'Then what happened?' It was Mrs Nix, and she hadn't even put her hand up.

CHAPTER SIX

He ran like nobody had ever run before. Twenty metres down the track was a red glow – the locomotive. The boy could make it if …

There was a snorting. The lion sniffed the carriage door, and then made its choice. Anything inside the carriage could wait. It was going for the runner.

The boy could hear his own breathing, hear his own footsteps, and hear the panting of the great creature behind. Nearer. It was getting nearer, but so were the steps up to the engine. He lunged for the handrail and dragged himself up, as the panting behind turned to a roar, and sabre teeth slashed at the air.

'So what happened to your brother?'

Grandpa didn't say anything. He looked exhausted now, and he started fiddling with his chair. It was twenty past three, and he needed to be up at the crossing.

Mrs Nix stood up. 'Well we must say a great big thank you to both of our guests this afternoon, Mr Purvis and …' There was a huge cheer. 'Mr Mahe.'

'That's Laila's granddad,' Laila heard someone near the back say, and, 'I go to her grandpa's house,' said a voice which could very well have been Annabelle's. Then she had a few golden seconds as a whole crowd ignored Mrs Thomas' clapping hands and turned to her in a blurb of sound.

But it was Scott who stopped the hubbub. He wanted to know.

'What did happen to your brother, Mr Mahe?'

Voice by voice the noise calmed into pure silence. Grandpa took a deep breath, and his eyes seemed to find Laila's again.

'He was killed, Scott.'

You could hear the hush.

'What, by the lion?'

'What kills more children than anything

else?' Grandpa asked the question in a whisper.

'Hippos.'

'No!' Grandpa pulled on his yellow Crossing Patrol uniform. 'Cars!' he said, and walked out and up to his crossing.

It took ages to get home with Laila holding Grandpa's hand and half of the class tagging on to hear what happened. Grandpa explained how his brother, in the locomotive, had managed to pull on a lever and release a cloud of steam that sent the lion scampering deep into the bush.

And then, when it was just Laila, he explained how he and Grandma had finally moved to England, and Baptiste had joined them to finish his schooling … but …

'He wasn't used to our traffic … It was half his fault and half the driver's …'

'So that's why you wanted to be a lollipop man.'

'I owed him. And if I can help just a little bit … well …'

They'd got to the door. Grandma opened it and Grandpa let Laila through first. He wanted a moment to himself.

'So what happened to the old lion?' Laila asked.

'He's still here,' Grandma said. And she gave Grandpa a big hug.

'Growl!' laughed Laila's lion. And in he stepped.

The Hunt

Written by
Kathryn White

Illustrated by David Dean

'Our art display for the Hindu festival has been ruined,' said the teacher sadly as she held up the art cloth for them to see.

The children gasped. Their work had been completely destroyed. The cloth had been dragged across the ground, and the beautiful deep-coloured dyes had smudged into one another so that no one could tell which image was Prince Rama and which was King Ravana.

'It's only a day until Dasara, the most important day of the festival,' went on the teacher. 'So we have no time to prepare anything else.'

All eyes looked at Sunil, a mischievous, lively boy of twelve, whose main pastime was practical jokes. Sunil blushed. 'It wasn't me,' he said indignantly. 'I wouldn't do something like that.'

The teacher sighed. 'Sunil, it is just the sort of thing you *would* do. I cannot think of another child who would do this.'

Everyone sat in shocked silence.

'It wasn't me, I promise. Why would I? It's stupid.'

The teacher frowned. 'Sunil, you said that at our last festival when you mixed maggots in your rice bowl and frightened poor Salesh to death.'

'But that was a joke.'

Bindy shot her hand in the air. 'What about when you put that snake in my bag,' she said, her brown eyes glaring angrily at Sunil.

'It wouldn't have hurt you,' Sunil said defensively.

Arun, Sunil's best friend, smiled inwardly, remembering the chaos Sunil's joke had caused.

'I hate snakes,' Bindy said quietly.

'And the egg,' Ashok piped up. 'You swapped my hard-boiled egg for a raw one.'

Sunil's face was turning hot with anger. 'It was just for fun,' he snapped.

'But it made a horrible mess,' Ashok said resentfully, 'and ...'

The teacher put her hands up to calm the unrest. 'Sunil, I think we would all find it easier to accept if you just admitted to it,' she said patiently.

Sunil sat rigid in his seat. 'It was not me,' he said defiantly.

There were groans of frustration from the class.

The teacher rolled up the artwork, disappointed. 'Every year we have offered something to celebrate Dasara, but we have no more dyes and no means of getting any more in time. If we can do one thing for this festival, it will be to behave honourably. Class dismissed.'

Sunil stormed out.

'Sunil, wait!' Arun called, running up to him. 'You've really blown it now,' he said with amusement.

Sunil looked hard at his friend. 'Arun, if you really believe that I ruined that stupid art piece, then you're an idiot.'

Arun bristled. 'Yes, I am an idiot,' he said. 'I've just realised who I've had as my friend.' And he walked away.

Sunil winced. First he'd been accused of

something he hadn't done, and now his closest friend had turned on him.

'They think it was me,' Sunil said angrily, storming into his grandfather's workshop. 'Someone ruined the art cloth for Dasara, and they all blame me.'

Sunil's grandfather kept his head down and continued working on his piece of wood. 'And why do you think they are blaming you?' he asked, suddenly looking up at his grandson.

Sunil shrugged his shoulders, then took his torch out of his pocket and began fiddling with the switch.

His grandfather grabbed his hand. 'Don't play around with that torch. You'll break it.'

'Do *you* think it was me?' Sunil asked.

His grandfather raised a brow. 'It's not me you've got to convince.'

Sunil marched off, annoyed that his grandfather had not been more sympathetic.

'Sunil …' his grandfather started.

Sunil turned in the doorway.

'Maybe you should think about why they are blaming you.'

Sunil went to speak, but his grandfather turned his back and Sunil knew that no more would be said on the subject.

As evening drew in, Sunil's anger and indignation grew. *He* knew he wasn't guilty. Somewhere in the village the culprit was getting away with it. He would have to find that culprit and make him or her own up. Before Dasara he would clear his name.

In the dark hours before dawn, Sunil crept out of his house. Armed with his survival kit – torch, rope and chewing gum he'd chewed and rewrapped so many times it no longer tasted like gum but just felt like it, he embarked on his search.

He moved silently, like a shadow, through the village and to the schoolhouse, where the art cloth had been laid outside to dry. He was wondering where to start his search, when suddenly he heard a noise.

It was far too early for anyone to be around the school. He crouched down in the shadows at the side of the building, bracing himself, certain he was about to come face to face with the offender.

He did.

Up on the school roof was a monkey, and something about it made Sunil smile. He had found what he was looking for. An immense relief swept over him, but he would have to catch the animal in order to prove his innocence.

The monkey disappeared over to the front of the roof. Instantly, Sunil popped his gum into his mouth, dashed out, and laid the silver wrapper on the ground. Speedily, he looped a special knot in his rope that his grandfather had taught him, placed the rope strategically over the wrapper, and then sank back into the shadows.

The monkey returned and spotted the silver foil glinting in the white moonlight. Its agile body swept down the side of the schoolhouse and up to the foil.

Tentatively, it went to take it.

At that moment, Sunil snapped on the rope and it slipped over the monkey's front leg. As the monkey pulled, the knot tightened.

'Got you!' Sunil exclaimed confidently.

But then the monkey yanked the rope and the end slipped from Sunil's hand.

'No!' Sunil cried, as the rope swept across the ground, dragged along by the terrified creature.

The monkey was fast, but Sunil dashed after it, stumbling on stones and twigs in desperate pursuit of the rope only just ahead of him, but always just out of reach.

The monkey ran far out of the village, and soon it was running into the forest, racing further and further into the trees.

But the monkey was small and beginning to tire. Sunil watched the rope getting closer with each step. Then, panting with frustration, he jumped, landing down hard on the end. The rope tugged under Sunil's feet, and he snatched it up, clutching it tight.

The monkey yanked and gnawed at the rope as Sunil drew it in closer. Two mischievous monkey eyes flashed bright from under a mop of rainbow-coloured hair. Up close, Sunil could now see that the monkey's head was bright blue, merging into mauves and reds. Its body was splattered with yellows and oranges, and its hair had matted into the strangest shapes.

'You must have had great fun playing on our art cloth!' Sunil laughed, tying the rope to a tree. 'And you can tug all you like, because when I come back to get you later, you will be tired and easily come home with me,' he said triumphantly.

As Sunil turned to go, the monkey jumped and shrieked, yanking angrily at the rope. Sunil looked back. 'You've caused me so much trouble,' he told the animal. But then he began to think of the trouble he had caused with his tricks in the village. It was no wonder they blamed him for the ruined art cloth ...

Sunil was on his way home, the captive monkey some distance behind him, when he suddenly stopped. He began to realise that he was alone in the forest – in the dead of night. Fear began to creep in. The moon lit up the forest and cast shadows across his path. Sunil felt uneasy.

As he continued walking, the hair on his arms prickled and Sunil sensed danger. It was as though he was being watched.

Sunil spotted a tree full of good climbing branches and began clambering up to get a safer view. It was a huge tree trunk, and it took all his strength to reach the first big overhanging branch. He was only just in time, for into the clearing sauntered a tiger.

Sunil gasped, wondering how long it had been tracking him. He crouched breathlessly on the thick branch, looking down at the pacing predator. She was beautiful. Somehow Sunil thought her a she. A deadly, graceful she.

She prowled, almost purring. But then the sound changed to a low grumbling that gathered momentum, and became a deep, dark growl. She could smell him, sense him. She knew he was there, but could not yet quite pinpoint where he was hiding.

Suddenly, her strong head looked up into the branches of the tree. Her eyes flashed like fire in the moonlight. She had him in her sights. Sunil's whole body stiffened in the horror of her gaze. Then she sidled off.

Sunil gripped the branch, tensely waiting for the tiger to circle the tree.

Every rustle in the forest seemed to be magnified and pierced through him as he clung on, wondering if she would be prepared to make the climb up – to claim her prey.

She reappeared from behind the tree and rose up on her hind legs. Sinking her large claws into the trunk, she darkly roared her decision. 'Yes. I'm coming for you now.'

Sunil recoiled. This was it. She would close in for the kill.

His stomach churned. He couldn't imagine a worse way to go – devoured in the forest where no one would ever find him.

Sunil imagined his friends and family back in the village, talking about him. 'Ah, it's one of Sunil's foolish jokes!' they'd say. 'He's just trying to scare us. Let's enjoy the peace while we can! He'll be back soon enough.' Only he would never be back, and they would never know what really happened.

He choked, wanting to cry out, but he knew that no one was there, only her, his hunter.

Sunil's heart began to race. He *couldn't* give in. He *wouldn't*. He wasn't going to just disappear. He had been able to catch the culprit – if he was going to prove his innocence, he had to survive.

He fumbled desperately through his pockets, searching for his precious torch. It had a good strong beam. His grandfather had saved so hard to give it to him as a special gift, and had proudly demonstrated the quality and strength of its light.

It just might work. It had to work.

He edged in closer to the trunk, balancing precariously on the branch, all the while searching shakily for the torch. He pushed his fringe out of his eyes; it was soaking with perspiration.

By now, the tiger had made another full circle of the tree and was preparing to mount her attack.

Sunil felt the torch dig into his leg. He wriggled, painfully levering it free. His breathing was shallow and rapid with terror.

The tiger stood below, calmly looking up, assessing her prey. Her white-lined face illuminated large and fierce in the moonlight.

Sunil kissed the end of his torch. 'Oh, grandfather,' he whispered. 'Let it work for me.' He closed his eyes momentarily and prepared himself, knowing his response to her attack had to be calm and precise.

He aimed the torch straight down, but kept it switched off. He wondered if the beam would be powerful enough to scare her. It was all he had.

He saw her graceful outline emerging from the undergrowth, sweeping in smaller and smaller circles around him.

Then she seemed to move away, and stood silently pawing at the ground, as if digging for something she'd found. But within a second, she'd jumped like a flash of lightning, and was halfway up the tree trunk.

Sunil gulped in terror at the speed of her advance, and locked himself rigid to the branch. He heard her clawing, moving with ease and precision, closer and closer.

Sunil's sweaty hand clenched the torch. He was panting noisily, unable to control his terror, unable to breathe properly. He flicked the switch on the torch.

Nothing happened.

He stared into the glass. It remained dead and lifeless. His eyes bulged in panic as he gazed, horrified, at the dull bulb, and then at the tiger's face, as it came level with his branch.

'Aaaaahhhhh!' Sunil screamed. And he hit out with the heavy metal torch.

The tiger's paw swiped up and caught his hand. It drew blood.

Sunil yelled out in pain and desperately shook the torch. 'Grandfather, help me!' he cried, as he gave it one last frantic shake.

Click ... on came the brilliant, piercing white torch light.

'YAA! YAA! YAA!' Sunil shrieked in terror at the top of his voice. 'YAA! YAA!' he bellowed, as he flashed the intense beam of light straight into the tiger's startled red eyes.

She froze, momentarily clinging in one position.

Sunil flicked the torch switch – on, off, on, off, keeping it fixed firmly, directly, painfully at her eyes.

'YAA! YAA!' he screamed, moving the beam as close to her eyes as he dared.

She turned her head sideways and roared.

Sunil kept on yelling and tormenting. Then he heard her claws scraping back down the trunk as she released her grip, and the thud of her paws as she half twisted, half jumped on to the soft ground below.

'YAA! YAA! YAA!' Sunil shouted, pursuing her with the light.

Confused and startled, she roared, and then dived off into the bush.

Sunil looked down, his dark, frightened eyes scanning the base of the tree. She had gone. It had worked.

Sunil looked up at the moon, repeating his call like a mantra, 'YAA! YAA! YAA!' The sound rolled off his tongue, loud at first, but then softer, gentler, faster, as he tried but could not stop the tears washing down his hot face.

His whole body ached and the cut on his hand was throbbing painfully. He felt hot and sweaty, but shivered at the thought of what might have happened.

As dawn began to break, Sunil climbed slowly back down the tree. He wrapped a large leaf around his cut and went back to collect the tied monkey.

When Sunil approached the village, the sun was beating down. Proudly, he held the rope, marching in with the colourful, obedient monkey at his feet.

His grandfather was sitting outside. He had been waiting through the night. And when he saw Sunil, his face lit up with pride.

Mr Hasbini's Garden

Written by
Elizabeth Laird

Illustrated by Tim Clarey

The boy was in the hospital office when the fighting started.

'Who are you looking for? What was his name again?' The clerk began to leaf without interest through a stack of files.

'Ramzi, I told you,' the boy said. 'He was at the secondary school. The one that was bombed. He's sixteen.'

'Didn't you come in here a few weeks ago?' the clerk said, looking up with a frown of irritation. 'I told you then that we'd had no boy of that name here.'

'But he might have been brought in later,' the boy said. 'Please. Please look.'

With no warning and with deafening force, a shell exploded near by. The clerk disappeared under his desk as fast as a mouse bolting into a hole.

The boy darted to the door and out of the building. He began to run, terrified of being inside in case the building collapsed around him.

The street was empty. Bicycles lay where people had thrown them down as they had dashed for cover. But the boy preferred to take the risk of being caught in the battle to the terror of being inside. He ran low to the ground, as fast as a hare, ducking and diving to make himself a harder target.

Shouts and explosions ahead made him swerve down a side alley. He ran fast, on and on, making for the edge of town.

At last he saw ahead the open road running through sun-baked fields and groves of orange trees. His pace slackened.

'Safe,' he thought, the word pounding in his head like the blood pounding through his heart. 'Safe, safe, safe here.'

Then, on the road ahead, he became aware of a low, steady roar. The boy screwed his eyes up against the blinding sun. He could make out a group of tiny specks in the distance, growing infinitely slowly but with awful steadiness as they approached. The pulse-beat in his head changed.

'Tanks,' it went, 'tanks, tanks, tanks.'

He looked round for a place to hide, and saw, a little way back from the road, a familiar pair of corrugated-iron gates opening into a walled compound. Through them he caught a glimpse of flowerpots laid out in rows under the shade of some ancient olive trees and he ran towards them.

Mr Hasbini, ignoring the familiar rumble and stutter of fighting two miles away in the town, had been squatting on the hot hard ground in the middle of his

nursery garden slicing geranium stems and
sticking them into pots full of freshly
watered soil. He stood up, grumbling as his
knees creaked, then pushed back his broken
straw hat and scratched his bald head as he
surveyed his long rows of pots.

'I'm a silly old fool,' he remarked to his pigeons, who were dozing through the midday heat in their cages under the shade of an old fig tree. 'Why do I bother? Who wants pot plants when there's a war on?'

He raised his head as he heard a distant rumble and frowned.

'Still miles away,' he said, 'but coming this way. I'd better close up in case.'

He was about to go and shut the gates when the boy ran through them into the compound. Mr Hasbini picked up a spade and shook it at him.

'Get out of here!' he shouted.

'It's all right,' panted the boy. 'It's me, Sami. You know me, Mr Hasbini. I used to come here with my dad to buy plants …'

'Sami? Mr Faris's son?' Mr Hasbini looked at the boy in astonishment.

'We've got to get out of here,' the boy said, dancing with impatience. 'There are tanks coming up the road. We'll be trapped!'

'And where do you suggest we go?' Mr Hasbini had rested his spade on the ground and was leaning on it. 'Up the road, into the battle in the middle of town? Or down the road towards the tanks?'

'Across the fields, through the orchards …'

'Don't be daft, boy. They're mined. No, we're going to stay here. Safest place to be. The tanks won't bother us. They're making for those hotheads up in town. Stop jumping up and down. You're giving me a headache. Tell me what on earth you're doing here on your own? Where are your parents?'

The boy shook back his tousled black hair and hitched up his trousers, which had grown too loose on his scrawny waist and fell in folds over his torn trainers.

'They went to my grandma's village, but I ran away. I've been on my own for weeks. I can't go till I've found Ramzi.'

'Your older brother? How did you come to lose him?'

'We were at school when it was bombed. The whole building collapsed. I got out all right, but Ramzi … He *must* have escaped! I *know* he did! But no one will believe me. Everyone just says …'

'Checked the hospitals, did you?' said Mr Hasbini.

'Yes. He's not in any of them.'

'In that case …' Mr Hasbini began.

'I know what you're thinking,' interrupted Sami, his newly broken voice suddenly high-pitched with anger, 'but it's not true! Plenty of boys got out. I saw them. There was shooting everywhere just after the bomb, and I ran away. I hid for hours till the fighting stopped, and when I went back I couldn't find Ramzi. I went home, and Dad said we had to go to the village, but I wouldn't go. I've been hunting and hunting …'

His voice shook and he wiped his forearm across his dirt-smeared face. Mr Hasbini stopped looking at him and squatted down among his flowerpots.

'What are you doing?' said Sami after a while.

Mr Hasbini dusted earth off his hands and sliced through another geranium stem.

'Taking geranium cuttings, of course. Didn't they teach you anything at school? These bits of stalk will grow into new plants. They'll be a picture next year.'

'Huh! Next year!' The boy squatted down beside him. 'We'll all be bombed to bits next year.'

'You probably will be if you keep on running round town in the middle of a civil war,' remarked Mr Hasbini. 'But these cuttings will still grow. It won't make any difference if we're dead or not. They'll just put out roots and leaves and turn into brand-new plants.'

'So what?' Sami picked up a geranium leaf and crushed it between his fingers.

'Stop that! Where's your respect for nature?'

'I don't care about nature. Nature's a waste of time.'

'A waste of time?' Mr Hasbini cast his eyes up to heaven. Do you know which side's going to win this war?'

'Our side is. My dad says …'

'Rubbish. Nobody's going to win. Have you seen that supermarket that was bombed last year? There are trees growing right through the tarmac in the car park, and grass and flowers sprouting all over the ruins. Nature's going to win this war, that's what. Nature always wins.'

'Listen. The tanks are coming,' said Sami, lifting his head.

'Never mind the tanks. They don't mind us,' said Mr Hasbini. Carefully, he pushed another geranium stem into the waiting earth.

Sami picked up the knife.

'Can I do one?' he said.

'Yes, but take care. Don't bruise it. Look, I'll show you …'

They both jumped suddenly as a burst of automatic rifle fire, coming from the direction of the town but quite close by, ripped through the air. Mr Hasbini struggled quickly to his feet.

'That was close! Quick, help me shut the gates!'

Sami was at the gates in an instant, clanging the first one shut. Mr Hasbini ran after him, his stiff legs working as fast as they

could. The tanks had nearly arrived outside the nursery garden, their huge caterpillar wheels clanking over the tarmac, but they stopped at the sound of gunfire, and their still-deafening engines were idling.

'Would you believe it! Those madmen are attacking the tanks!' panted Mr Hasbini as he shut the second gate and plunged the bolts home.

For a moment, they both relaxed. The nursery garden looked so peaceful, enclosed in its high wall. Except for the pigeons, who were fluttering with fright in their cages, it was almost impossible to believe that a battle was about to break out just outside.

But the ambush was only a few hundred metres away. Sami could even hear the men's voices as they broke cover; frantic questions and hoarse shouts of command.

'Can't stay here,' said Mr Hasbini. 'Gate's too flimsy. Bullets'll rip right through it,' and he began to run again, gasping for breath, towards the small concrete shed in the middle of the garden.

Automatically, Sami followed him. Then he saw where Mr Hasbini was going.

Not inside, he thought. Not trapped inside!

He looked round desperately. His
instinct was to run, but there was nowhere
safe to go. The pigeons were flapping their
wings and pecking violently at the wire of
their cages. Sami ran to them.

'Sami! Come here! What are you doing?'
Mr Hasbini shouted, but Sami did not listen.
He was fumbling with the latches of the
cages.

'Get out! Fly away!' he shouted as he
wrenched the doors open. 'You'll be
trapped, you stupid birds! Get out!'

The pigeons, more terrified than ever,
fluttered away from him into the backs of
their cages.

'Sami! Over here!' called Mr Hasbini. Sami looked round. Mr Hasbini was not inside the shed but behind it, crouching against its concrete wall.

The noise of the battle was deafening now. Sami could not see the men running down the road directly outside the compound, but he could hear the clatter of their feet and the sharp cracks of their rifles as they let off rounds of automatic fire. He felt the dreadful trembling weakness of terror engulf him as he dropped down beside the old man.

'I'd rather be outside at a time like this,' said Mr Hasbini. 'If I'm going to die, I'd rather do it with the sky above me, looking at my garden.'

Sami nodded. In spite of the heat, he was shivering. 'I was in the science lab when the roof fell in,' he said. 'I was near the window. I only just got out. I couldn't find Ramzi. He was in the library. I was …' He stopped, his lips trembling, then went on again. 'I've been hunting for three weeks, going round the hospitals, going to his friends' places, looking everywhere he might have run to if he was really scared.'

Mr Hasbini grunted. 'Why are you so sure he's still alive?'

'He's got to be! How can I be alive, and not Ramzi?'

With a deafening bang, a mortar hit the ground on the far side of the shed and exploded, splintering flowerpots and throwing earth and cuttings in all directions. Sami flinched, and covered his head with his arms.

There was a moment of eerie silence, as if the whole world was waiting. And then the tank opened fire. The 120mm shell flew over the compound wall with a deafening roar, screamed across the garden and ploughed through the wall on the far side with a bang that seemed to make the very air shake, and set the echoes flying.

Sami and Mr Hasbini had shrunk into themselves. They were squatting against the concrete wall of the shed with their arms tightly wrapped round their knees, making themselves as small as possible. Sami rocked backwards and forwards, and in the silence that followed the explosion, Mr Hasbini heard him whimpering. Not knowing what to say or how to comfort him, he began awkwardly to pat his shoulder, tears running down his own weather-beaten cheeks.

'Ramzi's dead, isn't he?' Sami said at last. 'You think he's dead.'

'Yes,' said Mr Hasbini.

Sami looked at him as if he was seeing him for the first time.

'We'll all be dead soon. What does it matter?' he cried suddenly, jumping to his feet. 'Why bother to take cover? What's the point? Kill me too, go on, get me too!' and before Mr Hasbini could stop him, he had run out from the shelter of the concrete wall and was standing unprotected in the open garden.

'Go on! Shoot me!' he shrieked at the sky, and he flung out his arms, put his head back and shut his eyes.

Nothing happened. Quietness had suddenly fallen. The battle outside was over. The only sound was the rumbling of the tanks' great caterpillar wheels as they started rolling on again up the road towards the town.

Sami opened his eyes.

'I'm alive!' he said aloud. 'Ramzi's dead, and I'm alive.'

He felt very tired and a little dizzy. He sat down on the ground.

'You certainly won't be alive much longer if you go on doing that kind of thing,' said Mr Hasbini disapprovingly as he came out from behind the shed. 'Scared me more than the tanks.'

He looked round his garden. The shell had blown a big hole in one wall and torn a branch off a tree, but most of the flowerpots still stood in their neat rows, and the pigeons, who had taken off and flown around in a high circle while the battle raged, had come back to peck and strut round the grain bowls in their cages.

'See what I mean?' said Mr Hasbini with a rare smile. 'Nature always wins.'

'I want to go home, to Mum and Dad,' said Sami suddenly, rising shakily to his feet.

'That's not a bad idea,' said Mr Hasbini. 'As a matter of fact, I think I'll come with you. I could do with a few days of peace and quiet. We'll wait till it's dark. It'll be safer then. In the meantime, let's eat. I've got some food in my shed. I expect you're hungry. Boys usually are.'

Sami nodded. Suddenly he was ravenous.

'I'll only stay away for a day or two, mind,' went on Mr Hasbini. 'I'll have to get back to mend that hole in the wall and do my watering, if the water's still turned on, and feed the birds.'

'I'll come with you,' said Sami. 'I'll help you.'

'Maybe,' said Mr Hasbini. He turned towards his shed. 'Come back in the spring, anyway. You won't believe your eyes. Those little bits of stalk will be great big geranium plants, all scarlet and orange and pink, and the cuts that made them will be quite forgotten. The world will be like a new place then. You'll see.'

The Eye of the Eagle

Written by
Ruskin Bond

Illustrated by Neil Reed

It was a high, piercing sound, almost like the yelping of a dog. Jai stopped picking the wild strawberries that grew in the grass around him, and looked up at the sky. He had a dog – a shaggy guard-dog called Motu – but Motu did not yet yelp, he growled and barked. The strange sound came from the sky, and Jai had heard it before. Now, realizing what it was, he jumped to his feet, calling to his dog, calling his sheep to start for home. Motu came bounding towards him, ready for a game.

'Not now, Motu!' said Jai. 'We must get the lambs home quickly.' Again he looked up at the sky.

He saw it now, a black speck against the sun, growing larger as it circled the mountain, coming lower every moment – a Golden Eagle, king of the skies over the higher Himalayas, ready now to swoop and seize its prey.

Had it seen a pheasant or a pine marten? Or was it after one of the lambs? Jai had never lost a lamb to an eagle, but recently some of the other shepherds had been talking about a golden eagle that had been preying on their flocks.

The sheep had wandered some way down the side of the mountain, and Jai ran after them to make sure that none of the lambs had gone off on its own.

Motu ran about, barking furiously. He wasn't very good at keeping the sheep together – he was often bumping into them and sending them tumbling down the slope – but his size and bear-like look kept the leopards and wolves at a distance.

Jai was counting the lambs; they were bleating loudly and staying close to their mothers. *One – two - three – four…*

There should have been a fifth. Jai couldn't see it on the slope below him. He looked up towards a rocky ledge near the steep path to the Tung temple. The golden eagle was circling the rocks.

The bird disappeared from sight for a moment, then rose again with a small creature grasped firmly in its terrible talons.

'It has taken a lamb!' shouted Jai. He started scrambling up the slope. Motu ran

ahead of him, barking furiously at the big bird as it glided over the tops of the stunted junipers to its eyrie on the cliffs above Tung.

There was nothing that Jai and Motu could do except stare helplessly and angrily at the disappearing eagle. The lamb had died the instant it had been struck. The rest of the flock seemed unaware of what had happened. They still grazed on the thick, sweet grass of the mountain slopes.

'We had better drive them home, Motu,' said Jai, and at a nod from the boy, the big dog bounded down the slope, to take part in his favourite game of driving the sheep homewards. Soon he had them running all over the place, and Jai had to dash about trying to keep them together. Finally they straggled homewards.

'A fine lamb gone,' said Jai to himself gloomily. 'I wonder what Grandfather will say.'

Grandfather said, 'Never mind. It had to happen some day. That eagle has been watching the sheep for some time.'

Grandmother, more practical, said, 'We could have sold the lamb for three hundred rupees. You'll have to be more careful in future, Jai. Don't fall asleep on the hillside, and don't read story-books when you are supposed to be watching the sheep!'

'I wasn't reading this morning,' said Jai truthfully, forgetting to mention that he had been gathering strawberries.

'It's good for him to read,' said Grandfather, who had never had the luck to go to school. In his days, there weren't any schools in the mountains. Now there was one in every village.

'Time enough to read at night,' said Grandmother, who did not think much of the little one-room school down at Maku, their home village.

'Well, these are the October holidays,' said Grandfather. 'Otherwise he would not be here to help us with the sheep. It will

snow by the end of the month, and then we will move with the flock. You will have more time for reading then, Jai.'

At Maku, which was down in the warmer valley, Jai's parents tilled a few narrow terraces on which they grew barley, millets, and potatoes. The old people brought their sheep up to the Tung meadows to graze during the summer months. They stayed in a small stone hut just off the path which pilgrims took to the ancient temple. At 12,000 feet above sea level, it was the highest Hindu temple on the inner Himalayan ranges.

The following day Jai and Motu were very careful. They did not let the sheep out of sight even for a minute. Nor did they catch sight of the golden eagle. 'What if it attacks again?' wondered Jai. 'How will I stop it?'

The great eagle, with its powerful beak and talons, was more than a match for boy or dog. Its hindclaw, four inches round the curve, was its most dangerous weapon. When it spread its wings, the distance from tip to tip was more than eight feet.

The eagle did not come that day because it had fed well and was now resting in its eyrie.

Old bones, which had belonged to pheasants, snow-cocks, pine martens, and even foxes, were scattered about the rocks which formed the eagle's home. The eagle had a mate, but it was not the breeding season and she was away on a scouting expedition of her own.

The golden eagle stood on its rocky ledge, staring majestically across the valley. Its hard, unblinking eyes missed nothing. Those strange orange-yellow eyes could spot a field-rat or a mouse-hare more than a hundred yards below.

There were other eagles on the mountain, but usually they kept to their own territory. And only the bolder ones went for lambs, because the flocks were always protected by men and dogs.

The eagle took off from its eyrie and glided gracefully, powerfully over the valley, circling the Tung mountain.

Below lay the old temple, built from slabs of grey granite. A line of pilgrims snaked up the steep, narrow path. On the meadows below the peak, the sheep grazed peacefully, unaware of the presence of the eagle. The great bird's shadow slid over the sunlit slopes.

The eagle saw the boy and the dog, but he did not fear them. He had his eye on a lamb that was frisking about on the grass, a few feet away from the other grazing sheep.

Jai did not see the eagle until it swept round an outcrop of rocks about a hundred feet away. It moved silently, without any movement of its wings, for it had already built up the momentum for its dive. Now it came straight at the lamb.

Motu saw the bird in time. With a low

growl he dashed forward and reached the side of the lamb at almost the same instant that the eagle swept in.

There was a terrific collision. Feathers flew. The eagle screamed with rage. The lamb tumbled down the slope, and Motu howled in pain as the huge beak struck him high on the leg.

The big bird, a little stunned by the clash, flew off rather unsteadily, with a mighty beating of its wings.

Motu had saved the lamb. It was frightened but unhurt. Bleating loudly, it joined the other sheep, who took up the bleating. Jai ran up to Motu, who lay whimpering on the ground. There was no sign of the eagle. Quickly he removed his shirt and vest; then he wrapped his vest round the dog's wound, tying it in position with his belt.

Motu could not get up, and he was much too heavy for Jai to carry. Jai did not want to leave his dog alone, in case the eagle returned to attack.

He stood up, cupped his hand to his mouth, and began calling for his grandfather.

'Dada, dada!' he shouted, and presently Grandfather heard him and came stumbling down the slope. He was followed by another shepherd, and together they lifted Motu and carried him home.

Motu had a bad wound, but Grandmother cleaned it and applied a paste made of herbs. Then she laid strips of carrot over the wound – an old mountain remedy – and bandaged the leg. But it would be some time before Motu could run about again. By then it would probably be snowing and time to leave these high-altitude pastures and return to the valley. Meanwhile, the sheep had to be taken out to graze, and Grandfather decided to accompany Jai for the remaining period.

They did not see the golden eagle for two or three days, and, when they did, it was flying over the next range. Perhaps it had found some other source of food, or even another flock of sheep. 'Are you afraid of the eagle?' Grandfather asked Jai.

'I wasn't before,' said Jai. 'Not until it hurt Motu. I did not know it could be so dangerous. But Motu hurt it too. He banged straight into it!'

'Perhaps it won't bother us again,' said Grandfather thoughtfully. 'A bird's wing is easily injured – even an eagle's.'

Jai wasn't so sure. He had seen it strike twice, and he knew that it was not afraid of anyone. Only when it learnt to fear his presence would it keep away from the flock.

The next day Grandfather did not feel well; he was feverish and kept to his bed. Motu was hobbling about gamely on three legs; the wounded leg was still very sore.

'Don't go too far with the sheep,' said Grandmother. 'Let them graze near the house.'

'But there's hardly any grass here,' said Jai.

'I don't want you wandering off while that eagle is still around.'

'Give him my stick,' said Grandfather from his bed. Grandmother took it from the corner and handed it to the boy.

It was an old stick, made of wild cherry wood, which Grandfather often carried around. The wood was strong and well-seasoned; the stick was stout and long. It reached up to Jai's shoulders.

'Don't lose it,' said Grandfather. 'It was given to me many years ago by a wandering scholar who came to the Tung temple. I was going to give it to you when you got bigger, but perhaps this is the right time for you to have it. If the eagle comes near you, swing the stick around your head. That should frighten it off!'

Clouds had gathered over the mountains, and a heavy mist hid the Tung temple. With the approach of winter, the flow of pilgrims had been reduced to a trickle. The shepherds had started leaving the lush meadows and returning to their villages at lower altitudes. Very soon the bears and the leopards and the golden eagles would have the high ranges all to themselves.

Jai used the cherry wood stick to prod the sheep along the path until they reached the steep meadows. The stick would have to be a substitute for Motu. And they seemed to respond to it more readily than they did to Motu's mad charges.

Because of the sudden cold and the prospect of snow, Grandmother had made Jai wear a rough woollen jacket and a pair of high boots bought from a Tibetan trader. He wasn't used to the boots – he wore sandals at other times – and had some difficulty in climbing quickly up and down the hillside. It was tiring work, trying to keep the flock together. The cawing of some crows warned Jai that the eagle might be around, but the mist prevented him from seeing very far.

After some time the mist lifted and Jai was able to see the temple and the snow-peaks towering behind it. He saw the golden eagle, too. It was circling high overhead. Jai kept close to the flock – one eye on the eagle, one eye on the restless sheep.

Then the great bird stooped and flew lower. It circled the temple and then pretended to go away. Jai felt sure it would be back. And a few minutes later it reappeared from the other side of the mountain.

It was much lower now, wings spread out and back, taloned feet to the fore, piercing eyes fixed on its target – a small lamb that had suddenly gone frisking down the slope, away from Jai and the flock.

Now it flew lower still, only a few feet off the ground, paying no attention to the boy.

It passed Jai with a great rush of air, and as it did so the boy struck out with his stick and caught the bird a glancing blow.

The eagle missed its prey, and the tiny lamb skipped away.

To Jai's amazement, the bird did not fly off. Instead it landed on the hillside and glared at the boy, as a king would glare at a humble subject who had dared to pelt him with a pebble.

The golden eagle stood almost as tall as Jai. Its wings were still outspread. Its fierce eyes seemed to be looking through and through the boy.

Jai's first instinct was to turn and run. But the cherry wood stick was still in his hands, and he felt sure there was power in it. He saw that the eagle was about to launch itself again at the lamb. Instead of running away, he ran forward, the stick raised above his head.

The eagle rose a few feet off the ground and struck out with its huge claws. Luckily for Jai, his heavy jacket took the force of the blow. A talon ripped through the sleeve, and the sleeve fell away. At the same time the heavy stick caught the eagle across its open wing.

The bird gave a shrill cry of pain and fury. Then it turned and flapped heavily away, flying unsteadily because of its injured wing.

Jai still clutched the stick, because he expected the bird to return; he did not even glance at his torn jacket. But the golden eagle had alighted on a distant rock and was in no hurry to return to the attack.

Jai began driving the sheep home. The clouds had become heavy and black, and presently the first snow-flakes began to fall.

Jai saw a hare go lolloping down the hill. When it was about fifty yards away, there was a rush of air from the eagle's beating wings, and Jai saw the bird approaching the hare in a sidelong drive.

'So it hasn't been badly hurt,' thought Jai, feeling a little relieved, for he could not help admiring the great bird. 'Now it has found something else to chase for its dinner.'

The hare saw the eagle and dodged about, making for a clump of junipers. Jai did not know if it was caught or not, because the snow and sleet had increased and both bird and hare were lost in the gathering snow-storm.

The sheep were bleating behind him. One of the lambs looked tired, and he stooped to pick it up. As he did so, he heard a thin, whining sound. It grew louder by the second. Before he could look up, a huge wing caught him across the shoulders and sent him sprawling. The lamb tumbled down the slope with him, into a thorny bilberry bush.

The bush saved them. Jai saw the eagle coming in again, flying low. It was another eagle! One had been vanquished, and now here was another, just as big and fearless, probably the mate of the first eagle.

Jai had lost his stick and there was no way in which he could fight the second eagle. So he crept further into the bush, holding the lamb beneath him. At the same time he began shouting at the top of his voice – both to scare the bird away and to summon help. The eagle could not easily get at them now; but the rest of the flock was exposed on the hillside. Surely the eagle would make for them.

Even as the bird circled and came back in another dive, Jai heard fierce barking. The eagle immediately swung away and rose skywards.

The barking came from Motu. Hearing Jai's shouts and sensing that something was wrong, he had come limping out of the house, ready to do battle. Behind him came another shepherd and – most wonderful of all – Grandmother herself, banging two frying-pans together. The barking, the banging, and the shouting frightened the eagles away. The sheep scattered too, and it

was some time before they could all be rounded up. By then it was snowing heavily.

'Tomorrow we must all go down to Maku,' said the shepherd.

'Yes, it's time we went,' said Grandmother. 'You can read your story-books again, Jai.'

'I'll have my own story to tell,' said Jai.

When they reached the hut and Jai saw Grandfather, he said, 'Oh, I've forgotten your stick!'

But Motu had picked it up. Carrying it between his teeth, he brought it home and sat down with it in the open doorway. He had decided the cherry wood was good for his teeth and would have chewed it up if Grandmother hadn't taken it from him.

'Never mind,' said Grandfather, sitting up on his cot. 'It isn't the stick that matters. It's the person who holds it.'